Contents

Welcome to this wonderful 2012 Annual! This year I've made sure that each page is filled with sparkles, snowflakes and Christmas magic. There are two brand new stories for you to enjoy, puzzles and activities to fill up those chilly winter days and some enchanting colouring and drawing to do. Have a jolly time!

Barbie xx

Pedigree

Published 2011. Pedigree Books Ltd, Beech Hill House, Walnut Gardens, Exeter, Devon EX4 4DH
books@pedigreegroup.co.uk I www.pedigreebooks.com

£7.99

Ellie one

A Christmas

Here's a special Christmas card from me to you. I've decided to fill my season's greetings with facts about me and my world, plus a few festive secrets that you might not know. Would you do me the honour of sharing some secrets about you? I'd love to know what you're getting up to this winter!

Barbie's Winter World

Height: 175cm   **Eye colour:** Blue

Hair: Long and golden blonde

Best friends: Nikki and Teresa

Pets: Sequin, Lacey, Taffy, Blissa, Tawny

Scrummiest winter food:
Aunt Millie's homemade chicken soup.
It warms you up from the inside out!

Most stylish accessory:
My pink furry snowboots – what's not to like?

Happiest hobby:
Skiing in the mountains. It's such a blast!

Funniest winter memory:
When Nikki, Teresa and I spent the night huddled under three duvets during a power cut. Even thought it was cold, I giggled right through to the morning!

The best Christmas ever was...
When I spent every moment with my three cool little sisters, Skipper, Stacie and Chelsea.

Ultimate winter warmer:
Sharing stories and candy canes round a log fire.

My favourite holiday snap:

This is me dressed up for a night at the panto with my fab friends!

card from Barbie

Fill in your Christmas card here.

My Winter World

Height: 1E5cm Eye colour: Bule

Hair: nutrull blond hair

Best friends: Sydnee maddy

Pets: cat Tigger

Scrummiest winter food:
flufey

Most stylish accessory:
my PINK skuf

Happiest hobby:
going to the skating
my PINK PomPom south

Funniest winter memory:
when my trens
am for a right   in side with
                   my famliy.

The best Christmas ever was...

when I got my bikd a
her wodrob
Ultimate winter warmer:

My favourite holiday snap:
(Stick your photo here or draw a picture of it)

Calendar cuties

BISCUIT

BISCUIT

JANUARY

M	T	W	T	F	S	S
						1
2	3	4	5	6	7	8
9	10	11	12	13	14	15
16	17	18	19	20	21	22
23	24	25	26	27	28	29
30	31					

My little Chihuahua loves playing in the snow, then cuddling up in the front of the fire. She's the perfect pup to share the new year with!

LACEY

FEBRUARY

M	T	W	T	F	S	S
		1	2	3	4	5
6	7	8	9	10	11	12
13	14	15	16	17	18	19
20	21	22	23	24	25	26
27	28	29				

Skipper's gorgeous rescue dog will do anything to get some attention. Scrunchie would be so much fun to take to a Leap Year party.

SCRUNCHIE

MARCH

M	T	W	T	F	S	S
		1	2	3	4
5	6	7	8	9	10	11
12	13	14	15	16	17	18
19	20	21	22	23	24	25
26	27	28	29	30	31	

Little Sutton brings style wherever he goes, just like his owner Nikki! He's the ideal pup to sniff out the best Spring fashions.

SUTTON

APRIL

M	T	W	T	F	S	S
						1
2	3	4	5	6	7	8
9	10	11	12	13	14	15
16	17	18	19	20	21	22
23	24	25	26	27	28	29
30						

Teresa's twin kittens are fun-loving little fluffballs! The cheeky pair would adore playing April Fool's jokes with you, then curling up for a cuddle.

TIKA & TIKI

MAY

M	T	W	T	F	S	S
	1	2	3	4	5	6
7	8	9	10	11	12	13
14	15	16	17	18	19	20
21	22	23	24	25	26	27
28	29	30	31			

Chelsea's snow-white bunny will only eat the finest food! She adores being taken to market to nibble on the new season's fruit and vegetables.

SLIPPER

JUNE

M	T	W	T	F	S	S
			1	2	3
4	5	6	7	8	9	10
11	12	13	14	15	16	17
18	19	20	21	22	23	24
25	26	27	28	29	30	

Taffy and her new clutch of pups make the summer so much fun! Who could resist playing with these little parcels of golden sunshine?

TAFFY

My friends and I are crazy about animals! We've put together a special calendar filled with pictures of our pat-table, perfect pets. Which is your favourite month? Use this page to remember the birthdays of all the people and animals that are special to you.

JULY

M	T	W	T	F	S	S
						1
2	3	4	5	6	7	8
9	10	11	12	13	14	15
16	17	18	19	20	21	22
23	24	25	26	27	28	29
30	31					

My kitten Blissa is just too cute! This little princess would love to be dressed up in glitter and bows then taken out to a glamorous summer ball.

BLISSA

AUGUST

M	T	W	T	F	S	S
	1	2	3	4	5	
6	7	8	9	10	11	12
13	14	15	16	17	18	19
20	21	22	23	24	25	26
27	28	29	30	31		

Stacie's always trying to get her fluffy hamster to get up and play! The little cutie could spend all summer stretching out in the sun.

RUGBY

SEPTEMBER

M	T	W	T	F	S	S
					1	2
3	4	5	6	7	8	9
10	11	12	13	14	15	16
17	18	19	20	21	22	23
24	25	26	27	28	29	30

My darling horse makes a beautiful September pin-up. She looks magnificent galloping into the sunset with her young colt at her side.

TAWNY

OCTOBER

M	T	W	T	F	S	S
1	2	3	4	5	6	7
8	9	10	11	12	13	14
15	16	17	18	19	20	21
22	23	24	25	26	27	28
29	30	31				

my birthday

Ryan's little dog Ruff fills October with super puppy attitude! Even though she looks strong and tough, she still gets spooked on Hallowe'en!

RUFF

NOVEMBER

M	T	W	T	F	S	S
		1	2	3	4	
5	6	7	8	9	10	11
12	13	14	15	16	17	18
19	20	21	22	23	24	25
26	27	28	29	30		

Ken's awesome dog Hudson has no trouble braving the autumn breeze! The canine crusader is determined to be a hero, just like his dad.

HUDSON

DECEMBER

M	T	W	T	F	S	S
					1	2
3	4	5	6	7	8	9
10	11	12	13	14	15	16
17	18	19	20	21	22	23
24	25	26	27	28	29	30
31						

My poodle Sequin is pampered, pretty and party-perfect! This adorable doggy is my best friend at Christmas and all year through.

SEQUIN

Friends Photo Call

This picture of my gal pals is in a special frame next to my bed. Do you like it? Nikki, Teresa, Summer and Raquelle are the best friends I could ever ask for – I always think of them before I go to sleep at night. Take a close look at the photo and then try and answer the quiz questions dotted around the page.

Point to the friend that's an international supermodel.

One of my closest pals is an amazing tennis player. Write her name in here.

barbie

Which girl has a soft spot for animals. Point to the friend that would never turn away a waif or stray.

GUYS GO Outside!

The boys have gone on a radical winter break to Canada – they're totally psyched about it! The minute that they get there, the gang are going to head outside to start ten days of extreme snow sports. Take a peek at the guys' ski passes to find out about their itinerary. It's totally out there!

SKI PASS

NAME:
KEN

FULL MOUNTAIN PASS

HEIGHT	EYE COLOUR	HAIR
188cm	Blue	Blonde

TOP WINTER SPORT
Snowboarding. I just gotta push those boundaries!

HOLIDAY AMBITION
To have a go at the bobsleigh. Totally awesome!

HOW I CHILL-OUT ON CHILLY NIGHTS
Tucking into a burger and fries whilst watching the sun sink behind the snow-topped trees.

THE BEST THING ABOUT THE TRIP
Having a blast with boy buddies!

nice

NAME:
STEVEN

FULL MOUNTAIN PASS

HEIGHT	EYE COLOUR	HAIR
183cm	Honey Brown	Dark Brown

TOP WINTER SPORT
Tobogganing. It's like riding nature's roller coaster!

HOLIDAY AMBITION
To spin the discs in the ski resort club.

boo boo

HOW I CHILL-OUT ON CHILLY NIGHTS
Logging onto my laptop and instant messaging Barbie with all the news.

THE BEST THING ABOUT THE TRIP
The hot chocolate – utterly scrummilicious!

NAME:
RYAN

FULL MOUNTAIN PASS

HEIGHT	EYE COLOUR	HAIR
190cm	Brown	Dark Brown

TOP WINTER SPORT
Skiing. I love the wind through my hair and the fresh mountain breeze.

HOLIDAY AMBITION
To write a soulful ballad about the falling snow.

good

HOW I CHILL-OUT ON CHILLY NIGHTS
Sitting by the fire inside our chalet, strumming my guitar.

THE BEST THING ABOUT THE TRIP
Taking some time out from the crazy world of high school.

THREE Super Sisters

I'm a very lucky girl – having three adorable kid sisters is the best thing ever! What I love best about Skipper, Stacie and Chelsea is that none of them is afraid to be themselves. Each of the girls has got a loveable and unique personality that makes them stand out from the crowd! When I'm not working my sisters come over to share sleepovers, giggles and games.

SKIPPER

I'm so proud of Skipper! Having a famous sister must be a lot to handle, but she takes the whole thing in her stride. Skipper is a smart cookie who's totally up on the latest technology and gadgets. She's connected 24/7, messaging her pals and posting on her video blog – she's got followers all over the world! Although she keeps it secret, Skipper is an amazing song-writer too.

DID YOU KNOW...

...that Skipper blogs under the nickname PJ Sherwood?

14

STACIE

My middle sister is bouncing with energy! Stacie is sweet, friendly and fun, and always on the go. Stacie is a superb sports girl and she's the captain of tons of teams. On the weekend she loves exploring new places and getting tons of fresh air. If ever I'm stressed about something, I know that a bracing walk and a good chat with Stacie will always blow my worries away!

DID YOU KNOW...

...that Stacie scored the most goals this season for her school football team?

CHELSEA

Chelsea is a baby sister with big ambitions! The cutie is already a famous child actor who's starred in tons of hit movies. Chelsea loves to act, sing and dance, but she's got lots to offer behind the scenes, too. She's loving and kind, and always ready to help out. When Chelsea comes over we often end up playing dress-up – it's so much fun putting on tiaras and sparkly heels, then clip-clopping round the house!

DID YOU KNOW...

...that Chelsea has played my sister on screen, too?

Winter WARDROBES

The weather outside is frightful, but I'm determined to look delightful! Can you help me pick the right outfits for my busy winter day? Draw a line to match the best look to each of the appointments in my diary.

A B C

D E

Today's Appointments

10.00
A walk in the park with Sequin and Taffy

11.30
Shopping at the mall

13.15
Fancy cocktail reception at a Hollywood hotel

16.00
Meet 'n' greet with my new movie director

18.30
Sleepover at Nikki and Teresa's

HAPPY Holidays

Don't you just love the holidays? The winter break has got to be the most special time of the year! I've filled this crossword with some of my favourite winter words. Use the clues to help you write each one into the grid.

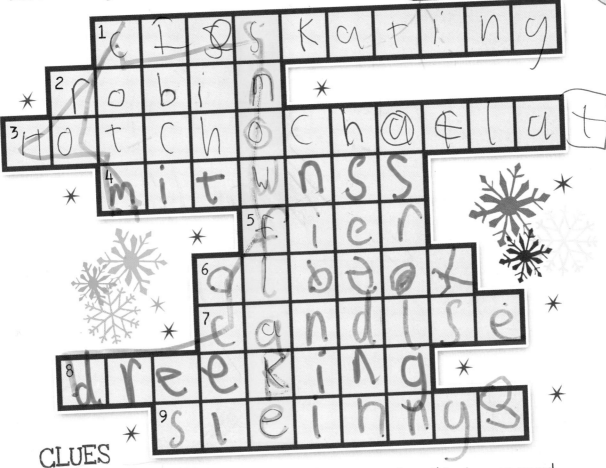

1. c e s s k a t i n g
2. r o b i n
3. H o t c h o c h a e l a t
4. m i t w n s s
5. f i e r
6. a l b a k
7. a n d l s e
8. d r e e k i n g
9. s l e i h n y s

CLUES

1. A graceful winter activity that takes place on a frozen rink.
2. A cute little bird with a puffy red chest.
3. A warm drink topped with marshmallows and cream.
4. A chilly sculpture to make in the garden.
5. A place to snuggle round with friends.
6. Knitted garments that warm up your hands.
7. Little wax columns that make the room cosy and bright.

8. Something to wrap round you on the coldest of nights.
9. A fast and fabulous winter past-time.

FOUND EVERY ONE?
Well done! Now read down the yellow panel to reveal one more magical winter word.

snoflaker

17

Dancing

DOT to DOT

This holiday season I decided to try a wonderful new activity! Can you guess what it is? Find a pencil and then carefully connect up the dots to reveal the picture of me ready to give it a go.

i can be...

4 ballaye techere

Barbie™ BEDTIME READING

Join Barbie and her friends in two great adventures! There's an amazing story of Princes and Princesses plus an all-action Christmas journey with an incredible ending!

STORY 1

Barbie™
PRINCESS
Charm SCHOOL

STORY 2

A Perfect Christmas

Turn the page and let storytime begin!

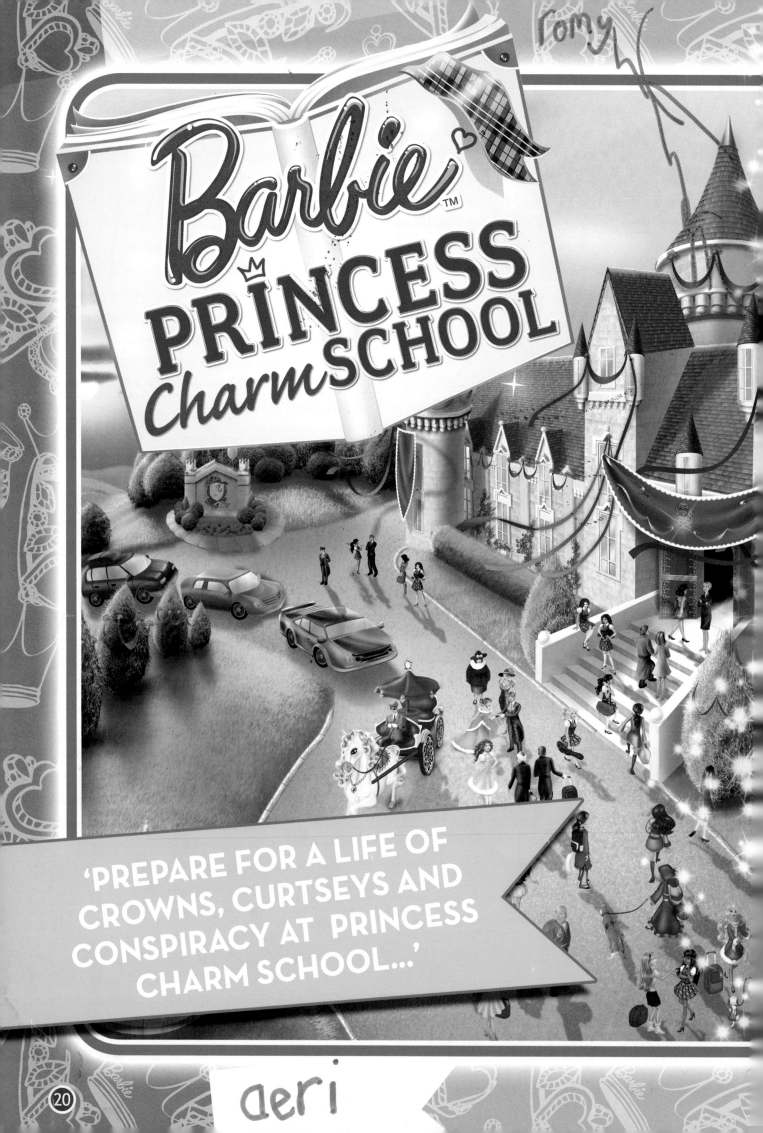

Blair

Isla

Hadley

Delancy

Dame Devin

Nicholas

Once upon a time...

...in a shabby urban house in the land of Gardania, a little girl called Emily sat glued to her favourite television show. She clapped her hands with glee as the presenters announced the start of the 144th Annual Procession to Princess Charm School.

"Emily!" called her mother. "I hope you're doing your homework and not just watching that parade!"

Emily grinned. She was much too enthralled by the glittering scenes on TV to concentrate on her books! Just then the front door opened and Emily's elder sister, Blair, walked in. Emily threw her arms around Blair's waist.

"Dance with me, Princess Emily," laughed Blair, noticing her sister's homemade tiara and thrilled expression.

"Let me get your tiara, Princess Blair," giggled Emily, pulling out another paper tiara and handing it to her big sis.

"I am soo not a princess," Blair sighed.

"Every girl's a princess," Emily said, putting the tiara on Blair's head.

Blair went to a jar in the kitchen and emptied her tips into it. The girls' mother was ill and so Blair was working as hard as she could to move the family to a nicer area of town with better medical facilities.

Their mother joined the girls on the sofa just as Princess Charm School Lottery began.

The family watched as the headmistress of Princess Charm School, a stern but wise-looking woman named Ms Privet, began to speak.

"At Princess Charm School those born to the royal life can unlock their princess potential."

Ms Privet explained that there are two types of students – royal-born girls who would become princesses and commoners who would become lady royals, trusted advisors to the princesses.

"Every year one ordinary citizen of Gardania wins a scholarship to the school," the headmistress continued. "She has the chance of changing her life and becoming a lady royal."

A haughty-looking girl called Delancy stepped up to draw the lottery. Her mother, Dame Devin, worked at the school. As the sister-in-law of the late Queen Isabella, Dame Devin still lived in Gardania's Royal Palace with Delancy. If Delancy graduated from Charm School she would become Gardania's next ruler.

Emily was on the edge of her seat as Delancy pulled a card out from the drum.

"Blair Willows."

"Woo-hoo!" Emily shrieked.

"You entered me?" Blair spluttered. She couldn't quite believe her eyes!

Emily admitted that she'd been entering her sister's name in the lottery for years.

At that moment the doorbell rang.

"Blair Willows?" growled a giant of a man. "Congratulations. I'm here to take you to Princess Charm School."

At first Blair refused point blank to go with the man, who introduced himself as Brock.

"I don't belong with a bunch of princesses and lady royals," she argued. "I'm a waitress! I have responsibilities here."

Her mother gently took her hand.

"It wasn't right of Emily to go behind your back," she said. "But this is a big opportunity."

So it was settled. Within minutes Blair found herself in a horse-drawn carriage on her way to Princess Charm School. She had nothing with her but the clothes she was wearing. Brock assured her that everything she needed would be waiting for her at school,

but she still felt very unprepared.

Blair tried to make herself look respectable by applying some of the make-up laid out for her, but suddenly the carriage swerved, smudging lipstick up her cheek.

"Oh great," she sighed. "I've already flunked carriage-riding."

Blair's worries were soon forgotten however, when she arrived at the imposing school. Inside, ancient tapestries adorned the grand stone walls. The sight of a fairy flying along the corridor made Blair bump into another student.

The surprised girl tried to say sorry, when something huge and hairy knocked her to the ground.

Blair had been floored by a fluffy golden retriever! The pet began to lick her lovingly.

"You're a good dog... Prince," Blair laughed, reading out his nametag. She was so busy petting her new friend she didn't hear the headmistress approaching.

"You must be Blair Willows," said Ms Privet. "We don't usually find our future lady royals sprawled across the floor."

Blair leapt to her feet. She didn't know whether to shake hands or curtsey!

"Hi," she waved uncertainly. "Sorry... he's just very sweet."

"He's normally shy," replied Ms Privet, showing Blair around the school.

"Emily would love this," Blair gasped, admiring the grand building.

As the pair walked, she explained how Emily had secretly entered her into the lottery. She had given Blair the chance to make a better life for her and their mum.

"Only 27% of the lottery girls make it to graduation," warned Ms Privet. "Do you think you are up to it?"

"I'll sure try," answered Blair, hoping that she wouldn't be expelled for knowing nothing about royal life.

Wham!

Suddenly Blair was hit in the chest by a flying fairy carrying a cupcake! The soft sponge splattered all over her.

"At your service, Miss!" said the fairy, wiping buttercream from Blair's shirt. Headmistress Privet introduced the clumsy sprite as Grace, Blair's personal princess assistant. Every student in the school had one.

"I shall leave you in her er... capable hands," Ms Privet said.

Grace apologised for the accident, telling Blair that cupcakes were the traditional welcome gift from princess assistants to their students.

The fairy fluttered in the air, showing Blair the way to her new locker. It was amazing! Tucked in alongside the usual books and school supplies were gem-encrusted mirrors, cosmetics and racks of glam accessories.

Grace threw a bottle of perfume to Blair. The new girl tried to catch it, but ended up accidentally spraying a passing student at the same time.

"You're...." said Blair, recognising the girl from the TV.

"Furious, that's what I am!" cried Delancy. "Let me guess, you're the lottery girl. Commoners like you don't belong here!" She flounced off, accompanied by Portia and fairy assistant Wickellia.

It wasn't a good start, but at least Blair's locker – which gave her a Princess Primp makeover – was fabulous.

And there was more good news. Blair's new room-mates were welcoming and super-friendly. Over lunch Isla and Hadley explained that they were trainee princesses with sprites called Harmony and Caprice. Hadley was sporty while Isla was really into music, constantly composing tunes in her head.

The girls had just got chatting when an announcement said that they had to be ready for the Starlight Welcome in just one minute. Thank goodness they had fairy assistants!

The Starlight Welcome evening was thrilling. Each student was presented with a decorative tiara, but warned that only those who graduated would earn a version made with real gemstones. Throughout the ceremony Prince lay at Blair's feet. He seemed to have taken a real shine to her!

Towards the end, Dame Devin stepped up to speak.

"This is my final term of teaching before my daughter takes over Gardania," she cried ignoring the fact that this still depended on Delancy graduating.

While Dame Devin droned on about her royal pedigree, Hadley and Isla leant over to whisper in Blair's ear. They told her about a legend that claimed Queen Isabella and her family hadn't all died in a car accident despite the official reports.

As the students lined up to bow goodnight to each other, Isla mentioned Gardania's Magical Crown. Blair was so fascinated she bumped heads with the person opposite her. Unfortunately it was Delancy.

"You again?" she yelled. "You're a walking disaster."

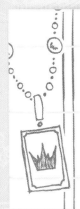

Blair had made an unfortunate enemy. In their posture lesson the next day, Delancy deliberately tripped Blair up while she was balancing a book on her head. The new girl tumbled into Isla sending her toppling into Hadley like a domino. Soon the whole class was sprawling across the floor!

"Stand up!" barked Dame Devin, eyeing Blair with disgust. "You are utterly unfit for royal life! I want you out of this class. You might think about whether someone from your station in life should stay in a place where you clearly don't belong."

Blair was very upset, but things just got worse. Delancy did everything she could to humiliate Blair in class and out. Only a special drawing from Emily showing Blair as a baby in a basket, reminded her why she had to stay.

"Emily loves the story of me being found on Mum's doorstep," Blair explained to her room-mates. "She adopted Emily a few years later."

No one noticed Ms Privet listening in the open doorway. Later that day the headmistress took Blair to one side. Dame Devin had recommended that Blair should be expelled, but Ms Privet had decided that she had princess potential.

"If you can dig deep and find the princess inside you," she smiled. "I've no doubt you'll graduate with your pick of any lady royal position."

Over the next few months under the headmistress' guidance, Blair began to develop grace, poise and perfect manners.

One afternoon there was a surprise in dance class – a group of Princes arrived!

As usual Delancy tried to ruin things for Blair, shoving her out of line so that she didn't have a partner. Luckily her cruel trick backfired horribly. Nicholas, the cutest Prince of all, showed up late and got paired up with Blair. Delancy was furious.

Prince Nicholas and Blair had an instant connection. The air crackled with chemistry as they floated around the dance floor. Delancy couldn't believe it – she liked Nicholas herself.

"You dance beautifully," Nicholas told Blair, as Dame Devin explained that the dancers would meet again at the Coronation Ball.

The Prince stooped to kiss Blair's hand.

"I shall count the moments 'til then," he murmured.

After class Blair, Hadley and Isla relaxed in their individual spa pools. The bubbles magically changed colour time and time again. That night all the students were due to visit Gardania's Royal Palace and so they wanted to look their best! As the girls lay back in the tubs, they discussed the mysterious question of the late Queen Isabella and Gardania's Magical Crown.

"It's said that the crown glows when placed on the head of the true heir of Gardania," marvelled Hadley. "It lit up on Queen Isabella's head at her coronation, but it hasn't been seen since then."

The sprites helped their charges out of the tubs and led them back to get dressed.

"Oh!"

When the girls got back to their dormitory, they discovered their uniforms ripped to shreds.

"What are we going to do?" Isla cried, picking up the torn pieces of cloth. "We're not allowed in class without our uniforms."

"We can't fail! Coronation Day's in just one week," wailed Blair. "How could this happen?"

"It was Delancy," decided Hadley. "She's the queen of the 'Make Blair Feel Inferior' Society."

"No one can make you feel inferior without your consent," replied Blair, remembering one of the headmistress's lessons. "We're princesses, right?"

"Not really, no," said Hadley. "We don't even have crowns."

"I'm not talking about crowns, I'm talking about character," Blair smiled. "The rule is we have to show up in uniform. Well, these just need a little alteration."

The plucky girl called in the princess assistants. It was time for the sprites to work their magic on the scraps of material.

At the palace that evening Dame Devin was just about to fail all three girls, when the grand doors opened. Blair, Hadley and Isla each looked fantastic as they strode in wearing revamped versions of their uniforms.

"Those aren't school-issued uniforms," shouted Dame Devin.

"Forgive me, Madame," replied Blair. "But they are made entirely from the material in our original uniforms."

Dame Devin shook her head, but Ms Privet agreed that there was nothing in the school dress code banning a beautiful restyle.

Once the other admiring students had simmered down, the headmistress told the girls that they were free to explore the palace.

Delancy followed Hadley, Blair and Isla, although she was careful to keep her distance. A few paces down the hall the friends came across a line of regal portraits.

"Look!" gasped Isla. "It's Blair."

Isla was pointing at a portrait of a girl wearing an exquisite tiara. She looked exactly like Blair!

"That's not possible!" Blair exclaimed. The plaque read 'Princess Isabella, age 18'.

The next picture was equally puzzling. It showed Queen Isabella, King Reginald, Princess Sophia and their loyal dog Prince!

"Look how sweet he is with that baby," Blair said. "He's such a little love."

"I always thought that the Princess Charm School dog didn't like anyone," Hadley whispered.

"But he sure likes you!" blurted out Isla, a look of realisation lighting her face. "Blair? Do you know when your Mum found you on her doorstep?"

"It was April 26th," Blair replied.

"It was the day that the royal family died in the crash," Hadley added. "And baby Sophia was one-year-old, the same as you. And her dog adores you..."

Blair gasped. Surely they weren't suggesting that she was really Princess Sophia of Gardenia?

"If it's true that would explain why Dame Devin and Delancy are so awful to you," nodded Isla. "You're the rightful heir to the throne!"

The girls were so busy laughing at the idea of Delancy being Blair's cousin they didn't notice their unwanted eavesdropper.

Later, back in the banquet room, Delancy was deep in thought. Her mother, Dame Devin, was irritated to see that she had also updated her uniform like Blair. For now she decided to ignore her daughter's rebellious behaviour and address the students.

"My daughter wants to make a declaration about how she'll handle things when she's crowned Princess next week..." she began.

Delancy looked utterly lost as her mother explained that once crowned she would take over the poorer, unattractive areas of town and bulldoze the homes to make room for beautiful tree-filled parks.

"People live in those areas!" Blair cried out in disgust.

"We don't have the money to just pick up and move."

Even the headmistress piped up to brand the idea disgraceful, but Dame Devin was unmoved.

After the other girls had left, Delancy confronted her mother. She told her about the portrait of Queen Isabella that looked so much like Blair.

"Does it have anything to do with baby Sophia?" she asked.

Dame Devin's lips curled cruelly.

"Are you sure you want me to answer that?" she sneered, her evil glare silencing Delancy. "I didn't think so. Keep following my lead and you and I will have the royal lives we so richly deserve. Get it?"

Isla and Hadley expected Blair to be devastated by Dame Devin and Delancy's dreadful plans for the kingdom. But when they got back to the dormitory their friend was bursting with determination.

"I'm ready," she announced.

"Ready for what?" Isla asked.

"To fight," Blair replied. "If Delancy gets on the throne she's going to ruin my family and this kingdom along with it."

Together the friends hatched a plan. They would prove that Delancy was not the rightful heir to the throne by finding Gardania's Magical Crown. When it wouldn't light up on Delancy's head, everyone would finally know the truth.

But first the girls had to find the Crown. They agreed to set off that night, when a fire alarm forced the whole school to evacuate the building.

While the students were outside, Dame Devin slipped into Blair's room. No one saw her hide a few pieces of jewellery amongst the friends' bedding. As they filed back indoors, Dame Devin began screaming.

"Arrest them!" she screeched. "They're thieves I tell you!"

Dame Devin accused Blair of stealing her gems to save her family from losing their home. Ms Privet had no choice but to allow Brock to search the girls' room. Blair, Isla and Hadley were horrified when the stolen jewels were discovered.

"We'll investigate this after the coronation ceremony tomorrow," said Ms Privet. "You'll remain locked up until that time."

All seemed lost as Brock handcuffed the girls and led them away.

"I'm so sorry," Blair told her friends. "Now neither of you will become princesses."

"Who needs a tiara anyway?" scoffed Isla, trying to make a joke. "They only make your head itch."

Suddenly a shout made Brock stop in his tracks – Delancy.

"I've got something else in mind for those prisoners. You may turn them over to me," she told Brock, adding that his orders would officially come from her once she was crowned in a few hours' time.

Brock gave Delancy the keys and strode off. Blair thought the girl had come to gloat, but instead Delancy started to unlock their handcuffs.

"Tell me," she begged. "Are you really Princess Sophia?"

"I don't know for sure, but I think so, yes," Blair said truthfully, rubbing her sore wrists.

"I think so too," replied Delancy. She handed the girls a map of the palace basement showing the way to the vault and the Magical Crown of Gardania.

"You have to find it," she urged. "Let everyone know the truth before the Coronation. Once I'm crowned, it's too late. Gardania will become mine for life."

"You don't want that?" Blair asked, surprised.

"I want what's right," the girl confessed, walking towards the Palace. "I have to get back, Mother will be looking for me. I'll leave a third floor window open. Use the map to find the vault in the basement."

The friends collected Grace and Prince and then crouched in the bushes to wait for nightfall. When darkness came they made their way towards the Palace.

Prince loyally distracted the guards at the gates, while Grace fluttered up to tie a rope on the roof. The girls used the rope to carefully clamber inside.

Luckily, Delancy's map was extremely accurate, helping the friends to quickly find the basement and vault. They managed to foil the heavy security by blowing face powder into the air to show up the alarmed laser beams. Blair had no trouble punching the right security code into the vault door – Dame Devin had simply used the date of her daughter's coronation. There, on a pillar encased in glass, was Gardania's Magical Crown.

"How do we get it out of the case?" Grace asked.

"You won't," snapped a voice. It was Dame Devin! Her two burly guards and Brock quickly had the girls overpowered once again.

"The Crown is mine Blair," she cackled. "You'll never be more than a poor lottery girl."

Dame Devin punched a new code into the security keypad, exiting the vault and locking them inside.

"We're sunk," sighed Hadley.

Blair wasn't ready to give up that easily. She pulled out her mobile phone and began fiddling with the wiring, linking it to the keypad on the wall. When the two connected, she asked Isla, the musical genius, to remember the tones from the keypad code. Isla hummed the exact tune and the door unlocked immediately.

The friends were free! They pelted out of the vault, through the basement and into the palace halls. In the throne room the royal judge had already begun presenting the successful princesses with their crowns.

"You are hereby dubbed Princess Miranda of Philadelphia," he said. "You are hereby dubbed Lady Royal Lorraine of Gloxinia. You are hereby dubbed Princess Portia of Narcissia..."

Soon it was Delancy's turn.

"Standing before me now is Delancy Devin who will govern our beloved and flourishing country, Gardania," said the judge.

Delancy desperately looked around for Blair.

Blair, it seemed, was nowhere to be seen and the crown was nearly on Delancy's head! Quick as a flash she insisted that proper princess protocol had not been observed.

"Before a new princess is crowned," argued Delancy. "The entire assembly must spin round seven times in honour of the seven hills of Gardania."

There was a delay of several minutes while the royal judge searched his book to check coronation protocol – just enough time for Blair, Isla and Hadley to burst into the throne room.

"Wait!" cried Blair, composing herself before striding confidently to the stage. "I am making a claim to the throne, because I am Princess Sophia, daughter of Queen Isabella."

There was a collective intake of breath. The judge dropped his coronation book.

"There is a resemblance," he admitted. Dame Devin went crazy.

"This is ridiculous," she screamed. "Sophia died seventeen years ago! Finish the Coronation and make Princess Delancy ruler of Gardania for life!"

In a blind rage she snatched the Magical Crown, but before she could place it on Delancy's head Grace whistled. Suddenly Caprice and Harmony fluttered under Dame Devin's feet, tripping her up.

The Crown flew into the air and Grace caught it neatly, placing it on Blair's head. The instant the circlet touched her golden hair it began to glow brightly. Blair's outfit was suddenly transformed into a magnificent coronation gown.

The crowd in the room gasped in astonishment when they saw that Blair was the real Princess Sophia, as did the millions of viewers watching TV coverage of the ceremony in their homes.

No one was more stunned than Emily Willows and her mother. In the blink of an eye, they had become royal relations!

"You useless child! Do you have any idea what you've done?" Dame Devin screeched as she lunged at Delancy. "I eliminated Queen Isabella so that you could be the Princess."

The malicious woman was so angry she had no idea that she had just confessed to murder on live TV. The royal judge instructed the palace guards to take her away.

"Blair, that is, Princess Sophia," asked Ms Privet. "Is there anything you'd like to say to your subjects?"

Blair stepped forward to make her first royal speech.

"I'm just a regular person," she said. "But Headmistress Privet is right when she says every girl has princess potential. I promise to always work hard and to be

just and kind. Thank you. It is an honour to be your princess."

The room erupted in cheers. But even in her finest hour Blair didn't forget her friends.

"Your Honour," she asked graciously. Would you please crown Hadley and Isla, Princesses of Delphinium and Acacia?"

Last of all, Blair decided that the person she really wanted as her lady royal was none other than her cousin Delancy.

Now it was time to party! The girls were thrilled to be joined by their favourite princes. Soon Blair was on the dance floor surrounded by her friends and the handsome Prince Nicholas, while Isla spun tunes from the DJ's booth.

Later that evening, Lady Royal Delancy announced that some very important visitors had arrived for the new Princess of Gardania.

Blair ran outside and saw the people dearest to her in the whole world climbing down from a horse-drawn carriage.

"Emily! Mum!" she cried. Emily was still wearing a paper tiara in honour of the occasion. She ran straight into Blair's outstretched arms.

"Welcome to our new home!" Blair told her sister and mother.

"Really?" gasped Emily. "We get to live in the Palace?"

Blair nodded and then added playfully. "I know it's not exactly the place we dreamed about..."

"Are you kidding?" shrieked Emily. "It's better than anything we ever dreamed about!"

"It is now the two of you are here," Blair laughed, hugging her family tightly.

Emily had one more question for her big sister.

"If you're a princess now, does that mean I'm a princess too?" she asked eagerly.

Blair swapped the real magical crown of Gardania with Emily's paper tiara.

"You've always been a princess," she smiled. She gently took her sister's hand and led her into her new home.

THE END

Barbie™

A Perfect Christmas

'Being together is what makes a perfect Christmas...'

Barbie

Skipper

Stacie

Chelsea

Christa

Rudy

A Perfect Christmas

"Has anyone seen my pink sparkly coat?" cried Chelsea, scampering into the bedroom with a wobbly pile of mittens, hats and cuddly toys.

"Knee pads, wrist guards, snow pants, snow shoes..." breathed Stacie. "Oh! My skates!"

Skipper wandered in next, capturing the chaos on her handheld movie recorder.

"PJ Sherwood here!" she announced into the webcam. "Counting down the minutes 'til we take off for New York City!"

Barbie trailed in after the girls, chatting into her mobile phone.

"A front row seat? Aunt Millie thank you so much!" she gasped. "We're packing now and can't wait to see you tonight. We'll call from the airport."

Barbie clicked the phone shut, then giggled. She and her three sisters were going to share a very special Christmas with their Aunt Millie. Every single one of them was totally over-excited!

As they packed their winter clothes, each of the girls thought about the fun they were going to have on the trip. Chelsea had her heart set on feeding the sea lions at the zoo, while Stacie was determined to spend the time ice-skating at the Rockefeller Ice Rink. Skipper had a special secret – her friend Zoe's band were going to perform a song that she had written at a Christmas concert in the city. Once Skipper had streamed their music live onto her website, the group was bound

to be a worldwide success!

Even Barbie had a Christmas wish. Aunt Millie had booked her a front row seat to see a top Broadway show!

Beep! Beep!

Barbie looked at her watch. The taxi had arrived to take them to the airport! The girls zipped up their suitcases and headed for the door.

"Let's go!" squealed Chelsea. "I just know that this is going to be the best Christmas ever!"

While the others loaded their cases into the cab, Barbie made a final dash back into the house.

"I mustn't forget these," she grinned, picking four colourful stockings off the mantelpiece. She popped the stockings into her case and then ran down to join her little sisters.

Barbie stared out of the aeroplane window, enchanted by the snowflakes shimmering in the night sky. It was definitely a chilly evening to be travelling! She leant forward to show Skipper, but her sis was plugged into a tune on her MP3 player.

"You should do one of your podcasts from here!" smiled Barbie, lifting up one of Skipper's headphones to get her attention. "You could even review the in-flight movie."

"Maybe later," frowned Skipper.

Barbie was going to chat some more, but Skipper pulled her headphone back on and maxed up the volume.

In the next seats, Chelsea and Stacie weren't getting on so well. Chelsea was trying to be as grown-up as her big sister, but to Stacie it just looked like copying. Before Barbie could break it up, the captain's voice came over the speaker system.

"Ladies and gentlemen, severe weather up ahead is going to force us to make an unscheduled landing in Minnesota," he announced. "Since we'll be delayed overnight, the airline will house everyone in local hotels."

"Minnesota is miles from New York," whispered Stacie. "Does that mean we won't get there in time for Christmas?"

Skipper, Stacie and Chelsea all looked heartbroken.

"We'll find a way to get to New York for Christmas," gulped Barbie. "Even if I have to drive us there."

A few hours' later, Barbie was steering through the Minnesota snowstorm in a rental car.

"We've been driving for ages," wailed Chelsea.

"That's because some of the roads are closed," explained Barbie. "With snow like this though, I don't think there'll be any planes going out tonight."

"Look!" cried Skipper. "There's a place called the 'Tannenbaum Inn' up ahead and it says it's got a vacancy."

Barbie smiled. "Perfect! We can stop here and get some rest before our flight tomorrow."

The sisters parked up and then rang the hotel's front doorbell. It sounded like jingle bells!

"Hello-ho-ho!" said a smiley lady in a pretty red dress. "My name's Christie Clauson and you're right on time!"

Christie led the girls into the lobby. The place was decked from floor to ceiling in stunning decorations. Hotel staff ran all over the foyer, wrapping gifts, polishing baubles and hanging treats on the Christmas tree.

A small girl called Holly Elif handed the sisters a mug of hot chocolate and a scrummy gingerbread man.

"It's just like Santa's workshop in here," beamed Chelsea. "You've even got elves!"

Christa winked. "Any place where people come together is one of Santa's workshops. Don't you think so?"

Christa showed the sisters to a cosy bedroom. While Barbie phoned Aunt Millie, Skipper checked out the weather reports on her laptop.

"Another snowstorm is going to bring major flight cancellations," she said, reading from the screen. "There's no way that our plane is taking off tomorrow."

Stacie's face fell.

"But we have to get to New York in time for our perfect Christmas!"

"Barbie promised," added Chelsea. "She said that we'd get there, right Barbie?"

Poor Barbie didn't know what to do. She couldn't see how they'd get on a flight, but she couldn't bear to let her sisters down.

"W-weather reports are wrong all the time," she stammered. "I promise we'll have the perfect Christmas."

When her sisters had drifted off to sleep, Barbie slipped out of bed. She wandered out to the hall window, her shadow bathed in the light of the silvery moon.

"I just wish that our Christmas will turn out right," she whispered.

Suddenly Christa tiptoed along the landing, concerned that her guest was OK.

"I promised my sisters the perfect Christmas," said Barbie. "And now in the morning I'm going to have to take it away."

Christa's eyes twinkled.

"The perfect Christmas isn't an object that you can take away," she smiled. "It's a feeling you get when you find joy in the people all around you."

Inspired by Christa, Barbie looked up at the moon and made a Christmas wish. But when she turned back to thank her, the hostess had disappeared.

"What's that?"

Barbie was surprised to see a trail of stripy candy canes dotted along the floor. She followed the festive treats across the landing, then down the stairs into the hotel lobby. The sound of sweet singing echoed round the Christmas tree.

"Skipper!" gasped Barbie, spotting her sister. "I had no idea that you could sing like that! What was that beautiful song?"

Skipper spun round, her face pink with embarrassment. She blushed even deeper as she explained that she'd written the song herself.

"You have to record that song," decided Barbie. "We're looking for music for my new movie. It'll be huge!"

"Just stop!" snapped Skipper. "I'm not a baby. I knew you'd try and take over and control everything!"

Barbie was shocked, but she could see how big a deal this was for Skipper.

"If you don't want my help, I won't help," she smiled, reaching for her sister's hand.

"Thanks," replied Skipper. "Zoe's band was planning to perform it tomorrow night in New York and I was going to podcast it. It was a really big deal, but we're not going tomorrow now, are we?"

Barbie felt her heart tug again.

"Maybe," she sighed. "But probably not."

"Sun's up!" shouted Chelsea, flinging back the bedclothes the next morning.

Stacie pointed out of the window and cheered.

"It's not snowing anymore!"

Barbie tried to smile, but she felt butterflies skip in her tummy as Skipper logged onto the weather report. It was not good news.

"The flight is cancelled," she sighed. "It snowed all night and the runways aren't clear."

"They could get clear in a couple of hours though, couldn't they?" asked Stacie, worried about her ice-skating trip.

Skipper shook her head. "More like a couple of days."

"But Christmas is tomorrow!" gulped Chelsea.

"I'll miss the special sea lion feeding."

Barbie thought of her show tickets. It seemed that they were all going to miss out on a perfect Christmas this year.

"What about Santa?" asked Chelsea, breaking into a sob. "How will he know how to find us?"

Barbie unzipped her suitcase and pulled out the girls' Christmas stockings.

"These will help him," she promised. "We'll hang them up at the window."

The girls brightened a little as they crowded round the glass.

"Look outside!" gasped Barbie. "Are those reindeer?"

Chelsea was already running to grab her coat. "We have to go and see!"

"Christa!" shouted Chelsea, tumbling through the snow outside the Tannenbaum Inn. "We saw reindeer. Santa's reindeer are here!"

"I don't know about that," said Barbie, running up behind with Skipper and Stacie.

"I believe you," smiled Christa. "Come and meet the reindeer!"

Their hostess led the girls to a field where eight adorable dogs in reindeer antler headbands were leaping around an agility course. As soon as they saw their visitors, they scampered over to say hello.

"They're so cute!" laughed Barbie.

"Every year we pick eight rescue dogs to play Santa's reindeer as part of our Canine Christmas," explained Christa. "So far every one of our rein-dogs has got adopted."

"Our dog Sequin would love that," smiled Skipper.

"Can I try taking the dogs through the agility course?" asked Stacie.

Chelsea clapped her hands. "Me too!"

Christa invited the two girls to give it a go. The dogs worked brilliantly, but Stacie and Chelsea couldn't help getting into another silly fight.

"You're a copycat," blurted out Stacie.

"I can't do anything without you tagging along."

"Be on your own, then!" snapped Chelsea.

The little girl stomped off into the snow. She felt lonely and hurt, until a sweet husky puppy pulling a sled ran over and licked her face. It had the name 'RUDY' printed on its collar.

"Can I get in your sled, Rudy?" she asked, climbing aboard. "Now dash away, dash away, dash away all!"

Rudy was trotting beautifully with Chelsea in his sleigh, when he suddenly spotted a squirrel jumping through the trees. He hurtled off after it, pulling Barbie's baby sister behind him!

"Woah!" screamed Chelsea. "Help!"

Barbie and Skipper heard the little girl's cries. They ran out of the agility arena with Stacie sprinting behind them. They could just see Chelsea clinging on to the sled.

Rudy hurtled down into a snowy valley, his little nose still fixed on the squirrel. Chelsea covered her eyes as the determined dog followed the creature onto a frozen lake.

"Oooh!' cried Skipper, falling onto her bottom.

Stacie pulled her back up. "Don't try to run normally," she explained.

"Take little steps and slide."

It totally worked! The three girls were soon skating after the runaway sled. They nearly had Rudy surrounded, when the cheeky pup bounded back onto the snow.

"Woohoo!" cried Chelsea, as the sled began to rocket down a steep hill.

Barbie spotted an abandoned sled propped against a tree.

"Come on!" she shouted. "We're going sledding too!"

Barbie, Skipper and Stacie climbed in for the ride of their lives. The three girls screamed with delight as they whistled down the hill, swerving left and right at a breakneck speed.

At last they landed with a **foomf!** - in a bank of fluffy white snow.

"Let's do that again!" giggled Chelsea, when Rudy finally stopped.

"You can't just take off like that," frowned Barbie. "You could have really gotten hurt."

But Chelsea wasn't listening. She'd just spotted a herd of real reindeer!

Chelsea was right. There, in front of a wooden barn, were eight reindeer! The girls watched, amazed as one silently began to approach them.

"He's beautiful," gasped Barbie, stroking the reindeer's soft fur.

Skipper's eyes danced. "They couldn't really be Santa's, could they?"

"Why not?" asked Chelsea. "Maybe they could."

The reindeer began to slowly walk back to the barn. As he walked the gentle creature kept stopping and turning back to the girls. It was as if he wanted them to follow him!

The sisters looked at each other and then slowly trailed behind.

"I guess this is where they live," decided Stacie, pointing up at the barn.

Chelsea couldn't help running up and peeping inside.

"Guys!" she squealed. "You have got to see this!"

The sisters gasped in surprise. The barn was stacked from floor to ceiling with presents – more presents than they'd ever imagined!

"Christa did say that she did a toy drive every year," said Skipper.

Stacie shook her head. "Could they really make this many gifts?"

"Maybe if they worked hard all year?" wondered Barbie.

The sisters decided to go back to the hotel and ask Christa about what they'd seen.

Climbing back up snowy hills took a lot longer than sledding down them.

"We've been walking forever," sighed Chelsea.

"This was all your fault," replied Stacie. "You wouldn't stop copying me!"

Chelsea picked up a pile of snow and threw it at her sister. Soon, the girls were in the middle of a massive snowball fight! Skipper wanted to hurry the pair along, but she and Barbie couldn't resist joining in too.

Rudy played in the snow as the sisters had the best fun ever. The girls tumbled around in the gorgeous white countryside, making snow angels and singing carols. When they finally collapsed red-faced and laughing, the sound of cool pop music began to echo round the meadow.

"Did you hear that?" said Skipper.

She followed the sound up to an old garage.

Inside, a band were rocking out to Christmas tunes. A guitar player called Brian waved at Skipper.

"I watch your video log!" he gasped. "You call yourself PJ Sherwood. It's awesome!"

Skipper smiled. "What about you? Do you have a website I can link up to?"

Brian's face fell. He explained that the band didn't have a site because they didn't have a singer.

"We play pretty great, but we won't get anywhere without a vocalist," he sighed. "It was really cool meeting you though."

"Good luck," smiled Skipper. "You guys are awesome."

The sisters waved goodbye to Brian and his band, ready to make the last trudge back to the inn. Barbie couldn't help but notice that Skipper looked thoughtful.

"Those guys reminded me of Zoe's band," she explained. "I still can't deal with losing the chance of them performing my song."

A fabulous idea popped into Barbie's head, but she bit her tongue. She'd learnt the night before how Skipper didn't like her taking stuff over.

Her sister grinned. "You totally want to give me some advice, don't you?"

"Why not podcast Brian's band tonight?" suggested Barbie. "They can play your song and you can sing it! We can ask Christa to hold a Christmas Eve concert at the hotel!"

"If I'm going to do this," replied Skipper, seriously considering it. "I don't want it to be a Barbie thing."

Barbie nodded. "If that's what you want, I'll leave it to you."

"You really think I can pull it off?" wondered Skipper.

"I know you can," answered Barbie.

Skipper raced back to the garage. She needed to see how Brian's band felt about a Christmas Eve debut with a new song and a new singer!

Brian and his band were thrilled with Skipper's proposal. The sisters marched back to the hotel as fast as they could.

Barbie spotted their hostess out on the veranda. Skipper ran up and explained her plan.

"I love it!" said Christa. "And I know exactly who to call to make sure everyone knows about it."

"The band and I will need somewhere to rehearse..." smiled Skipper, her eyes twinkling with excitement.

Christa nodded. "Use the basement. You can set up a stage out here for the show. Just ask me or the Elifs and we'll help!"

"We want to help too," piped up Chelsea and Stacie.

Barbie wasn't sure. "This is Skipper's thing..."

"How about the girls put on an opening act?" suggested Christa. "The audience would love an animal show with the shelter dogs."

"That's a great idea!" agreed Skipper.

Chelsea stared up at Barbie. Now everybody had a job apart from her.

"Barbie can make popcorn," decided Skipper. "Please...?"

Barbie smiled graciously. "If that's where you need me, I'm all over it."

Barbie went upstairs to call Aunt Millie, leaving Skipper and her crew to get to work. But when she popped down to check on them a little later, the production was in chaos.

"I'm so glad you're here!" cried Christa. "Skipper won't let us do anything, but she's

too busy rehearsing to let us help."

Barbie frowned, then wandered over to the animal area. Instead of working on their routine, Chelsea and Stacie were in the middle of another big fight.

"I'm not being mean!" snapped

Stacie. "I just think it's better if we do our own animal acts."

"I want to do a show together at the same time!" yelled Chelsea.

"Umm…" sighed Barbie. "I guess it's really up to Skipper."

Skipper stormed in, her head in a whirl. Chelsea and Stacie began bombarding their sister with questions.

"Not now!" she shrieked. "I need to sort tons of other stuff out first. I've got to do this myself, just like Barbie does."

Stacie glared at Chelsea. "See? Now you're in everybody's way!"

Barbie quietly took Skipper to one side to explain that even she needed help sometimes. Everyone was in such a fuss, it took a full five minutes for anyone to notice that Chelsea had stormed out into the snow.

Skipper led the way.

"We have to find her," she shouted. "We're sisters. Let's work together!"

The girls formed a search party, quickly discovering sleigh tracks in the snow.

"Chelsea must be riding in Rudy's sled again," said Skipper.

Stacie's heart thumped. "But it's getting dark outside!"

A dusting of snow started to cover Rudy's tracks, but Barbie had an idea. She led her sisters to the only place that Chelsea knew round here – the reindeers' home!

The girls pushed their way through the wintry weather, determined to get there fast.

A little while later, they finally saw the reindeers' stable up ahead. Rudy's sledge was propped neatly outside.

"Chelsea!" cried Barbie. There was her sister, curled up in a cosy nest of fresh hay.

"Hi guys," yawned Chelsea.

Barbie, Skipper and Stacie swept their baby sister into a tight group hug.

"I was thinking that one animal act is probably better than two," whispered Stacie. "I'm sorry."

Chelsea's face lit up. "You mean it?"

"She would mean it if there was going to be a show," sighed Skipper. "It's an hour 'til the performance. We'll never be ready."

"I feel awful," said Barbie. "You must feel like your whole Christmas is ruined."

Skipper shook her head.

"Are you kidding?" she laughed. "As long as we're all together, it's the perfect Christmas!"

The girls headed outside to stroke the reindeer one last time, but the herd had gone. Instead the moon glimmered above them, full, bright and beautiful. Each one of the sisters made a silent wish.

"Ho, ho, ho!" echoed a voice in the distance.

"Did you hear that?" gasped Barbie.

Skipper pointed down to the snow. Wide sleigh tracks curved in the moonshine then disappeared.

"They weren't here a minute ago," she marvelled.

"Guys!" called Stacie. "Look at this!"

The sisters followed Stacie up to the barn they'd visited the day before. Instead of being stacked to the rafters with gorgeous gifts, the room was perfectly decorated for a show. There was a stage,

curtain, fairy lights and Christmas trees.

"There are our stockings!" cried Chelsea. "They're filled with presents!"

Christa suddenly popped her head round the door.

"There you are," she smiled. "My uncle called me after he picked up all the presents in here. He thought this would be the perfect spot for a show."

"How did he do all this?" asked Stacie, her face full of wonder.

Christa gave the sisters a special smile and then turned to face Skipper.

"Forty-five minutes 'til showtime," she said. "Can you do it?"

"Not without lots and lots of help," replied Skipper, reaching for Barbie's hand.

Barbie grinned. "We'd love to."

Before they knew, it was time for the curtain to go up. The barn had a full house!

"We present the Cute-tastic Canine Choir!" announced Stacie and Chelsea.

The audience clapped as the rein-dogs and Rudy performed their tricks. The display was stupendous!

Barbie and Skipper were ready to greet the girls when they ran backstage.

"This is even better than New York," gushed Skipper. "Because you're all part of the show too."

"I'm still part of an animal show," agreed Chelsea. "But I got to do it with Stacie."

Stacie gave her a hug. "And I got to sled and play in the snow with all of you."

"And now I've got what I wanted too," added Barbie. "A front row seat for an incredible performance!"

Christa gave Skipper a friendly wave.

"It's time for you to sing your song!"

"Break a leg," whispered Barbie, running to take her place.

The house lights dimmed and Skipper stepped onto the stage. Brian's band started to play her song and the audience clapped their hands.

"This has been the perfect Christmas," sang Skipper. **"Cos I got to spend it with you!"**

Barbie's eyes filled with tears – Skipper had

written new lyrics especially for the show!

Over in the wings, Ivy Elif gave her the thumbs up. The tune was getting thousands of hits on Skipper's podcast, too.

Suddenly the music broke off.

"There's no way I can finish this song without some more help," smiled Skipper. "I'd like my three special sisters to join me!"

Barbie, Stacie and Chelsea rushed up on the stage, just as Aunt Millie walked into the barn. Somehow, she'd manage to wangle a place on one of the only flights into Minnesota!

The girls put on a magical performance. Thanks to each other they'd learnt that the perfect Christmas can happen anywhere, as long as you're sharing the joy of the season with the people you love. When the show was over, the revellers ran outside to enjoy the moonlight.

"Look at that!" cooed Barbie.

A stunning Christmas tree shimmered in the snow.

"It's incredible," smiled Aunt Millie. "But how did it get there?"

"It's Christmas magic," said Chelsea. "Christmas magic!"

The End

Charm School
CHALLENGE

DID YOU ENJOY YOUR VISIT TO PRINCESS CHARM SCHOOL?
I WONDER IF YOU'D MAKE A PERFECT PRINCESS?
MS PRIVET HAS SET A SPECIAL QUIZ TO FIND OUT
IF YOU WERE PAYING ATTENTION! FIND A PRETTY
PEN AND THEN TICK THE CORRECT ANSWERS.

1. THE PRINCESS CHARM SCHOOL LOTTERY ALLOWS...

A. One ordinary citizen to live in the palace forever ☐

B. One ordinary citizen to train as a lady royal ✓

C. One ordinary citizen to win a million pounds ☐

2. WHAT IS A LADY ROYAL?

A. A person trained and chosen to be advisor to a princess ✓

B. A lady-in-waiting who dresses the princess ☐

C. The princess's personal assistant at school ☐

3. WHAT IS SPECIAL ABOUT THE LOCKERS AT CHARM SCHOOL?

A. They have special security keypads ✓

B. They can magically give you a makeover ☐

C. They lead directly to your dormitory ☐

4. WHAT ROLE DO THE FAIRIES AND SPRITES HAVE?

A. They do all the cooking and baking ☐

B. They guard the crowns and tiaras ☐

C. They are personal princess assistants to the students ✓

5. WHAT SWEET TREAT MIGHT YOU EXPECT TO RECEIVE WHEN YOU ARRIVE AT SCHOOL?

A. A big bag of Princess Peppermints ☐

B. A yummy cupcake ✓

C. A stick of royal rock ☐

6. WHAT MAGICAL EXPERIENCE COULD YOU EXPECT IN THE SCHOOL SPA?

A. A manicure where your nails get instant polish ☐

B. An enchanted brush to scrub your back ☐

C. The bubbles in your tub to change colour ✓

7. HOW COULD YOU TELL IF THERE WAS AN IMPOSTER ON THE THRONE OF GARDANIA?

A. Their Magical Crown would not light up ✓

B. Their lady royal would turn into a frog ☐

C. Their gown would change into rags ☐

8. WHICH OF THESE IS NOT A LESSON AT PRINCESS CHARM SCHOOL...?

A. Gardening ✓

B. Poise ☐

C. Dance ☐

0-3 CORRECT ANSWERS

You're not quite at graduation level yet, but the good news is that you get to enjoy another term at Princess Charm School! Remember what Ms Privet always says, 'being a true princess is not about crowns, it's about character.' Why not show determination and re-read the story before re-taking this test?

4-7 CORRECT ANSWERS

Well done, you're well on your way to becoming a perfect lady royal. You've just a few more lessons to learn! Practice makes perfect, so head off to poise class and try walking the length of the room with a pile of books on your head. Now that's true grace!

9. WHO PRESIDES OVER THE ANNUAL CORONATION CEREMONY?

A. The headmistress ☐

B. The royal judge ✓

C. The existing King or Queen of Gardania ☐

8-10 CORRECT ANSWERS

Congratulations, clever clogs! You've passed with flying colours and have graduated Princess Charm School. Time to pick out your best gown and wash your locks before the coronation ceremony. You don't want a bad hair day when you're being crowned!

10. YOU'LL SURELY WANT TO ENTER THE NEXT LOTTERY AND VIEW THE PRINCESS PROCESSION ON TV! NEXT YEAR WILL BE THE...

A. The 144th annual lottery and procession ☐

B. The 145th annual lottery and procession ☐

C. The 154th annual lottery and procession ✓

Royal Portrait

PAINTER

Here's Blair all dressed up and ready for class! Do you like her revamped Charm School uniform and Princess Gardania Magical Crown? Create your own royal portrait by copying each square in the top grid into the matching blank panel below. When you've drawn Blair's picture, use felt-tips or crayons to make her jacket and jewels pop in shades of princess pink.

P.P.A. S.O.S.

Help! Blair's Personal Princess Assistant Grace has got lost in Gardania's Royal Palace! Can you trace your finger through the corridors and help Blair find her wayward Personal Princess Assistant? You'll need to look carefully – there's only one safe route in and out of the maze.

Start here!

Princess Picks

Blair wants to remember every little detail from her special coronation – it's not every day that a girl gets transformed into a princess! Stepping up as Princess Sophia made Blair feel very proud, but the most exciting thing was the thought of sharing it with her Mum and baby sister.

Take a close look at this stunning coronation photograph. Can you find all the little star images in the main picture? One of them doesn't belong in this scene, circle it with a bold crayon or pen.

A

B

C

D

Imagine that you are a princess and draw yourself in all your finery.

Charm School

CUPCAKES

At Princess Charm School, yummy cupcakes are the traditional welcome treat for all would-be princesses and lady royals. Poor Blair ended up wearing rather than tasting hers thanks to Grace's clumsy presentation skills, but she's tried lots more batches since!

Have you ever whipped up a tray of cupcakes? The smell of the little treats baking in the oven is divine! Ask a grown-up if you can give this simple recipe a try. It will make enough cakes for you and 11 of your friends.

You will need

120g plain flour
140g caster sugar
1 ½ tsp baking powder
A small pinch of salt
40g soft unsalted butter
120ml whole milk
1 egg
1/2 tsp vanilla extract

WARNING!

Always ask an adult before using sharp kitchen knives or the oven – it's important to be safe in the kitchen!

Cooking Instructions

1. Line a baking tray with 12 individual paper cake cases, then pre-heat the oven to 170°C/325°F/Gas Mark 3.

2. Click the paddles into a handheld whisk and then ask an adult to help you mix up the flour, sugar, baking powder, salt and butter in a deep bowl.

3. Gradually pour in half the milk and keep beating for a few more seconds.

4. In a separate bowl, stir the egg, vanilla extract and remaining milk together. Gently add this into the flour mixture, whisking until the cake mixture becomes smooth and creamy.

Cooking Instructions

5 Spoon the mixture into the paper cake cases so that each one is about two-thirds full. Ask your helper to put the tray in the middle of the oven for around 20-25 minutes. The sponges will be springy and golden-brown when they're ready.

6 Although it's tempting, leave the cupcakes to cool in the tray before you start decorating!

Perfect Party Cakes

There's all sorts of princessy ways you can decorate your cupcakes. All you need to do is spread on some pink icing and then get sprinkling! Here are some of our favourite toppings – which one will you choose?

Chocolate curls

Strawberries

Silver balls

Sugarpaste flowers

Mini cookies

Dolly Mixtures

Sweet!

Christmas COLOURING

Barbie
Skipper
Stacie
Chelsea

Thank you so much for sharing our wonderful Christmas story. Did you enjoy it? Find your brightest pens and then colour in the scene where my sisters and I first stepped into the amazing Tannenbaum Inn. When you've finished you could add your own stickers or sprinkle on glitter to add extra magic!

Christmas is perfect for me if I can share it with...

Christmas Stocking

My sisters and I agree that hanging up our stockings on Christmas Eve has got to be the most exciting time of the year! Do you have a stocking, sock or pillow case that you leave out for Santa? This little make-it will show you how to make another cute felt stocking to pin up by your bed or on the mantelpiece.

1. Put a sheet of tracing paper over this page and draw over the stocking template. Carefully transfer the template onto a sheet of white paper and cut it out.

2. Fold your piece of felt in half and then pin the stocking shape onto it. Ask for some help to cut two matching stockings out of the material.

3. Thread a needle and then neatly sew the stockings together, leaving the top edge open.

4. Snip off 8cm of coloured ribbon and stitch it in a loop at the top edge of your stocking.

5. Now your stocking is ready to decorate! Sew on buttons, bright beads or sparkly sequins and then hang your Christmas creation somewhere special.

You will need:

★ Tracing paper
★ Pencil
★ White paper
★ Scissors
★ Pins
★ Coloured felt
★ Matching thread
★ Needle
★ Ribbon
★ Buttons, beads and sequins to decorate

Ask a grown-up to help you before using sharp scissors, pins or needles.

You could even draw a festive pattern on your stocking using fabric pens!

Gift Tag Game

I've bought and made some gorgeous gifts this year for my family and friends – I can't wait to see their faces when they open up their parcels! Something seems to have gone wrong with the gift labels – the names on the tags are in a complete jumble! Will you help me address each one properly? Please write the correct name neatly on each gift.

EKN

NATU EILMIL

1. ken

2.

KINIK

KEPSIRP

3. niki

4.

YARN

EAREST

5. ryan

6.

Superstar SCRIBBLES!

When I travel the world, I'm often asked for my autograph. I love signing my name for my fans! I've been told that the large loops in my 'B's mean that I'm theatrical and confident. Have you ever wondered what your signature says about you? Imagine you're a movie star like me and sign your autograph in the frame below.

Now turn the page upside down to reveal what your autograph reveals about your personality.

★ If your writing slants forward, you're an outgoing high-achiever who is top of the class.

★ If you sign in printed capital letters you are selfless and very loyal, but you can lose your temper at times.

★ If your letters slant backwards you have self-control and keep your emotions in check.

★ If you've underlined your name you have fantastic self-confidence, but can sometimes be a little selfish.

★ If you've written your full name you have firm views on life and can be stubborn, but you're also blessed with bags of will power.

★ If you've used hearts or smiley faces to dot your i's, you are a fun-loving person who doesn't take themselves too seriously.

★ If you signed your first initial and surname you're a deep, sensitive type who can be shy and reserved.

★ If your letters don't touch you're impulsive and artistic, but if they connect you're more logical by nature.

P IS FOR...
Pretty Words

I've never noticed it before, but so many of the things I love begin with the letter 'p'! Ten of my favourite 'p' words are hidden in this wordsearch grid – see if you can you draw a circle around every one. The words could be running backwards or forwards, up or down or even diagonally.

P	A	P	U	P	P	I	E	S	P
R	T	E	Y	M	U	G	D	E	P
I	M	P	Y	J	A	M	A	S	E
N	Z	I	J	S	P	C	X	I	A
C	H	N	H	T	H	K	L	K	R
E	Y	K	Q	E	I	S	W	O	L
S	W	S	S	P	O	N	I	E	S
S	V	I	Y	F	C	J	K	Z	J
V	G	N	I	R	E	P	M	A	P
P	A	L	S	T	R	B	R	D	C

Word Perfect!

Can you think of three of more words that start with 'p'? Write them here.

1. preety
2. poo
3. elot

- [✓] PALS
- [ ] PAMPERING
- [ ] PETS
- [ ] PEARLS
- [ ] PINK
- [✓] PONIES
- [✓] PYJAMAS
- [ ] PEACHES
- [✓] PRINCESS
- [✓] PUPPIES

A SUPER, SURPRISING
Saturday!

Cast

BARBIE

CHELSEA

SKIPPER

KEN

STACIE

TERESA

One Saturday afternoon was chillaxing in her bedroom, when an instant message from popped up on her laptop. had been trying to book ice hockey tickets as a surprise for , but the game was a complete sell-out. and felt sad – was going to be so disappointed!

Just then, a call came through from and , inviting to go skating at the park. The invite gave a wonderful, wintry idea!

Can you read this mini-story out loud? Every time you come to a picture of me, my friends or my sisters, look at the cast list and say the name underneath.

me
plitee

She text , telling her to bring  and  to the park at 5pm. A few more calls to her pals and it was

all sorted.

When  got to the park, she

was in for a big surprise!  and her

friends had arranged for them to have

a big game of ice hockey, followed by

pizza all round.  gave  and

 a hug – playing hockey was

so much more fun than just watching

from the stands!

75

Style me
PLEASE!

I've got an invitation to the Snow and Sparkle Ball at the City Hall this evening, but I can't decide what to wear! Will you be my stylist? Take a look at the outfits in my closet, then colour in the star below the one that suits me best.

Pink cocktail dress with contrast heels

Frilled and fab sequin frock

Simple black dress with silver sparkles

Belted purple gown with frou frou underskirt

Silver sequin top with sweet layered skirts

Answers

Pg 10-11: FRIENDS PHOTO CALL

Raquelle is an international supermodel.
Summer is an amazing tennis player.
Teresa has a soft spot for animals.
Nikki has a passion for fashion.
Raquelle and Barbie both have blue eyes.

Pg 16: WINTER WARDROBES

10.00: A walk in the park with Sequin and Taffy: **C**
11.30: Shopping at the mall: **D**
13.15: Fancy cocktail reception at a Hollywood hotel: **A**
16.00: Meet 'n' greet with my new movie director: **E**
18.30: Sleepover at Nikki and Teresa's: **B**

Pg 17: HAPPY HOLIDAYS

```
I C E S K A T I N G
R O B I N
H O T C H O C O L A T E
S N O W M A N
    F I R E
  G L O V E S
  C A N D L E S
B L A N K E T S
  S L E D G I N G
```

Pg 18: DANCING DOT-TO-DOT

i can be...
A Ballet Teacher

Pg 60 - 61: CHARM SCHOOL CHALLENGE

1. B	2. A	3. B	4. C	5. B
6. C	7. A	8. A	9. B	10. B

Pg 63: P.P.A. S.O.S.

Pg 64 - 65: PRINCESS PICKS

C

Pg 71: GIFT TAG GAME

1. KEN   2. AUNT MILLIE   3. NIKKI
4. SKIPPER   5. RYAN   6. TERESA

Pg 73: P IS FOR....PRETTY WORDS

```
P A P U P P I E S P
R T E Y M U G D E P
I M P Y J A M A S E
N Z I J S P C X I A
C H N H T H K L K R
E Y K Q E I S W O L
S W S S P O N I E S
S V I Y F C J K Z J
V G N I R E P M A P
P A L S T R B R D C
```